CREATED BY BERNICE CHARDIET

THE MAGIC FISH RAP

WRITTEN BY JON CHARDIET
ILLUSTRATED BY SAM VIVIANO

SCHOLASTIC INC.
New York Toronto London Auckland Sydney

ISBN 0-590-45859-0

Copyright © 1993 by Chardiet Unlimited, Inc.
Book Design by J. C. Suares. Illustrations © 1993 by Sam Viviano.
All rights reserved. Published by Scholastic Inc.
CARTWHEEL BOOKS is a trademark of Scholastic Inc.
RAP TALES is a trademark of Chardiet Unlimited, Inc.

12 11 10 9 8 7 6 5 4 3 2   3 4 5 6 7/9

Printed in the U.S.A.   23

First Scholastic printing, March 1993

HERE WE GO
HERE WE GO

Once
upon a rhyme,
a long time ago,
out by the sea
where the cold
winds blow,
a fisherman lived
with his wife
in a shack.

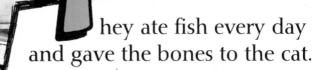

They ate fish every day and gave the bones to the cat.

The fisherman's wife wasn't happy at all.
See, for her, cookin' fish was never a ball.
They had fish for breakfast, fish for lunch,
with the cat in the corner goin'

CRUNCH
CRUNCH
CRUNCH

They had fish for dinner, fish for dessert.
They had fish until their nostrils hurt.
They drank fish shakes and ate fish pie.
They ate fish so much they wanted to die.

One day the funky fisherman
went to the shore
to see if he could catch some more.
He strung up his pole,
put a worm on the line,
and sat on a rock
for a long, long time.

He sat on the rock,
then he got a strong bite.
"It's gotta be big
'cause it's puttin' up a fight."

His arms started aching,
and the pole almost broke.
And he pulled so hard
that he started to choke.

Then all of a sudden,
the fish was in his lap.
The tail hit his head
and went

FLAP FLAP FLAP!

He was almost crushed
'cause the fish was so big –
it was twice the size
of an ordinary pig.

It was a big ol' flounder,
bug-eyed and fat.
It looked like a blanket
and was just as flat.
The fisherman looked it
right in the eye –
and this big flat fish?
Well, it started to cry!

"Please don't eat me!
Don't eat me, I say.
Just throw me back in the water.
Lemme swim away.
I'm really a prince.
A witch made me like this.
Throw me back!
I won't taste good in a dish."

The fisherman jumped up
and started to scream.
He thought the talkin' fish
was just a bad dream.
He said, "I would never put
a prince in a stew.
I'll throw you back in the water
if it's what I have to do."

He put the fish in the water
and it started to sink.
It left a long trail of blood
and swam away in a wink.
The fisherman ran as fast as he could
to his little brown hut
made of stones and wood.

He told his wife the story,
and she gave him a look.
Then he showed her the blood
on his fisherman's hook.
She said, "Go back to the water
and ask for a wish from this
enchanted, talking flounder fish."

He said, "What could we wish for?"
She said, "What? Are you nuts?
For years we've lived in this one-room hut,
eating fish every morning, noon, and night.
A nice house with a garden
will set things right."

So the funky fisherman
walked to the ocean,
before his wife could start a commotion.
He said, "Oh, Flounder–Prince,
        Oh, Prince of Fish!
        My wife's gonna kill me
        if I don't get a wish!"

The fish came up,
and the water turned blue.
The fish said, "What do you want me to do?"
The man gave his wish, and the fish said,
        "Go back.
        You'll see that you no longer
        live in a shack."

The man ran home
and what did he see?
A house big enough for families three!
There were cows in the garden
and chickens in the field,
fruits and vegetables for every meal.

For about three weeks, everything was fine.
They ate cookies and cake
and had a good time.

No one ate fish, not even the cat.
They fed the kitty steak and chicken fat.

But then one day, his wife said, "Dear,
I don't think that I'm happy here.
I want a castle with a big stone tower.
Go tell your fish. He has the power."

The fisherman said he didn't want to go.
But his wife didn't understand
the meaning of "No!"
With his heart feelin' heavy
and fear on his mind,
he went to the seashore one more time.

He got to the water, and the water was brown.
There was wind – and storm clouds all around.
He said, "Oh, Flounder–Prince,
Oh, Prince of Fish!
My wife's gonna kill me
if I don't get a wish!

If she can't have a castle,
my life's gonna end.
Please give her a castle
made of stone, my friend."

The fish said, "Done,"
and the man ran home.
And what did he see?
A castle of stone!
A castle with servants,
horses, and a moat.
A moat big enough
to hold a ship that could float.

The man held his breath
and went inside,
and there was his wife,
beamin' with pride.
She was dressed in a gown
made of satin and silk,
and at her feet, the cat
was bathing in milk!

KITTY

MILK

B

ut then one morning, his wife awoke.
And what she said
made the fisherman choke.
She said, "Fly back to the fish
like a bird on a wing.
And tell your buddy
you want to be King."

"I don't wanna be King," he said.
"Understand?"
She said, "Do it, 'cause
it's part of my personal plan!"
"I won't be King," he said.
"Kings are mean. "
"If you won't be King," she said,
"then I'll be Queen."

Pretty soon the man ran down
to the edge of the ocean, his face in a frown.
He said, "Oh, Flounder–Prince,
        Oh, Prince of Fish!
        My wife's gonna kill me
        if I don't get a wish!"

The water turned black,
and a storm was high.
Then the fish came up
and looked the man in the eye.
The fish said,
        "What does your wife demand?"
The fisherman said,
        "To be Queen of the land!"

The fish said, "Done,"
and went back down.
The fisherman sighed
and turned around,
walked back to the castle,
and almost died.
It had turned to gold,
and it was twice as high.

People were bowing
to the brand–new queen.
The fisherman thought
he was in a dream.
His wife, the queen,
looked very sinister.
And so did the cat,
who was now the prime minister.

She had armies and servants
and gold galore.
The cat wore so much gold,
he couldn't move from the floor.
The queen moved her finger,
and they carried him there.
And he sat by her side
in a little wooden chair.

This went on for about a week.
The man had to kneel just to speak
to the queen, his wife,
in her chair of gold.
The cat was now so heavy, he had to be rolled.

T hen one morning the queen woke up,
took a drink of water
from her golden cup,
and said to the cat,
        "Get my husband in here. "
Her husband said,
        "What is it, dear?"

        "Dear? I'm the QUEEN," she said.
"Your highness to you!
I've decided this kingdom
just won't do!
Go down to the fish,
go now, and run!
And tell him I want power
over the sun.

"Control of the sun, the stars, the moon.
Now run to the fish, and do it soon.
Tell him I'll have it, or you will die.
Tell the fish I want the power . . .
or I'll make him fry!"

The fisherman walked out
with an aching head.
His heart was sad,
and his feet were like lead.
He went to the rock
and said, "Oh, Fish!
My wife's gonna kill us
if she doesn't get her wish."

The sky turned black,
and the water went wild,
and the storm could be seen
for a hundred miles.
Thunder rang, and lightning streaked,
and from the black, foamy water
he heard the fish speak.

"What now?" it said.
"What more can she get?
She's Queen and she's not happy yet?
I gave her a castle made of gold.
I tell you, fisherman, your wife's too bold!"

The fisherman said, "She wants the power
over moon, sun, and stars at every hour!

The sun, the wind, the earth's motion.
She also wants power over the ocean."

The water went crazy,
the sky turned red,
and in a very deep voice
the fish-prince said,

"Your wife's very greedy,
and you are weak.
Go back to her now,
unless it's death you seek!"

The man turned around and ran away.
The storm almost took his life that day –
the lightning was striking all around.
He got home and fainted,
fell down on the ground.

The castle was gone;
in its place was a shack.
The wife and the cat
were hiding out in back.
Gone were the gold
and the diamond rings,
the thrones and all the expensive things,
given and taken by a power divine.
What was left was a pole
and some fishing line.

So they went back to eating fish every day.
And the fisherman's wife
had nothing to say.
They had fish for breakfast, fish for lunch
with the cat in the corner going

CRUNCH
CRUNCH
CRUNCH!